T0197523

Baby needs Pants

By

Dyan Beyer

To order additional copies of this book, contact:
Xlibris
844-714-8691
www.Xlibris.com
Orders@Xlibris.com

ISBN: Softcover 978-1-6641-9945-3
Hardcover 978-1-6641-9946-0
EBook 978-1-6641-9944-6

Print information available on the last page

Rev. date: 11/18/2021

Dedicated to my grandson, Paul Dolman Beyer.

Welcome to our family and to this wonderful world!
You are the sweetest little guy who's smile
won me over the first time I saw you!
Love you more than words can say!

Proverbs 22:6:

Train up a child in the way he should go,
even when he is old he will not depart from it.

Other children's books by

Dyan Beyer

Under Angels' Wings

Baby Boy Bear

Baby Grace is Here!

Once upon a time there was a baby born in the fall named Paul. He had everything he needed. He had a Mommy and Daddy. He had a Gram and Grandpa. He had a cat named Rat and a dog named Cat! He had chickens and chicks, roosters and pigs! Baby Paul had a house with lots of land, horses and cows and plenty of ducks who quacked very loud! He had a garden filled with corn that was planted before he was born! He lived on a farm with a little red barn. He had plenty of toys, enough for many boys! And he had lots of love from God up above!

Gram asked Paul's Daddy what else was needed for the laddie.

"Baby needs pants! That's all that's needed for laddie!" Said Daddy.

Somewhat surprised, taking a stance, Gram asked, "Baby needs pants?"

"Yes...he needs pants, even though we are blessed!" Daddy confessed.

"Grandpa and I will get him pants in all colors, not just gray, if that's okay?"

“What kind of pants should we get our precious little lamb?” Asked Gram, tickling Baby Paul’s tummy, trying to be funny!

“Hmm, let me think….should we get him pants to keep him warm? Or should we get him pants that are long? Should we get him pants that our worn but, certainly, not torn! Should we get him pants for when he is tall or for now when he is small? Or should we just get him pants so he can dance?”

Suddenly, Paul smiled and grabbed Gram’s finger. She said, “I think I know what makes you smile! It’s words that rhyme, something you will learn to do in time.”

Baby Paul smiled for awhile, knowing that he would get pants so he can dance!

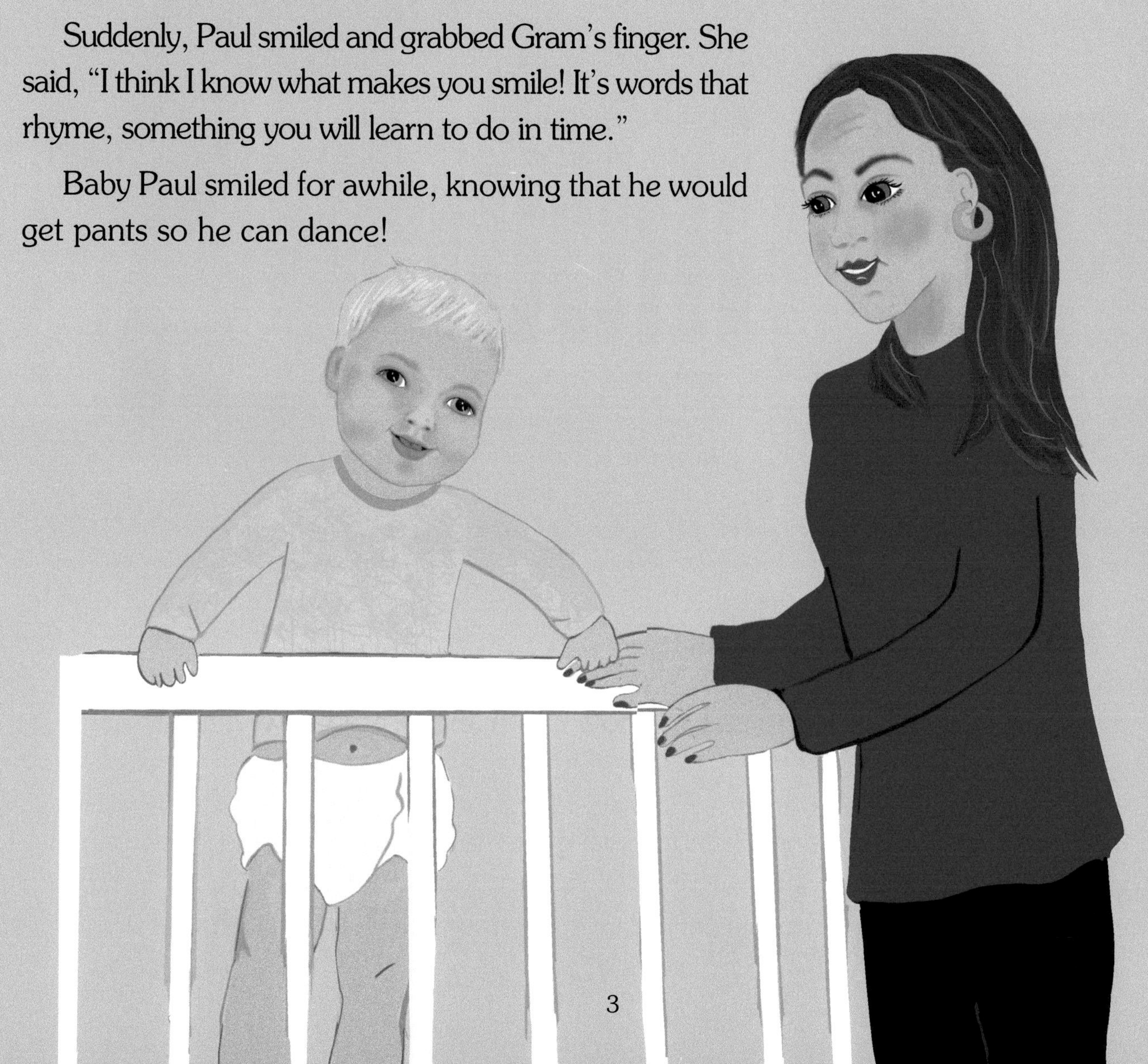

Daddy said, “Baby needs pants and now Gram and Grandpa will get you pants so you can dance!”

Mommy said, “Gram and Grandpa will go to the store and bring back pants that you will adore!”

Gram and Grandpa drove through the muck, hoping to get to the store without getting stuck. Down the path, blocking the way, was a cow looking like she was taking a bow!

Grandpa got out of the truck and said to the cow, “Why are you blocking the road when we are trying to go!”

The cow mooed and mooed, Gram tried too, “Please let us through! We’re on our way on this lovely day to buy baby pants so he can dance!”

Grandpa tried pushing the cow but she stood still in the mud chewing her cud.

Grandma pleaded, “Please move off the road! If only you were a toad, it would be easy to get you to go! But don’t you know, you are still in the middle of the road and baby needs pants so he can dance?

Grandma pushed the cow’s rump and she moved over the bump! With a loud moo and a little shake- a- do.

Grandma and Grandpa was once again on their way to get baby his pants so he can dance.

They came upon a horse who thought he was the boss! His neck swung around when he saw Gram and Grandpa on the road but he continued to nay, sway and stay in the way.

Grandpa had an idea to use some FORCE to move that HORSE. He pulled his tail but that seemed to fail!

Gram moved close to the horse and asked, “Do you know why we need to pass and to do it fast? Because baby needs pants so he can dance! We need to go quick!” Then the horse gave Gram a smile and a lick!

At last, the horse moved fast to let them pass!

It wasn't long before they saw the fawn right before dawn. She sat on the route tempting Grandpa to give her a boot!

Grandpa said, "Oh no not again! Please move out of the way, we can't stay all day!"

The fawn looked away, only wanting to play.

Gram thought quick and tossed up a stick. The fawn, named Blanche, jumped up to chase that branch. Gram and Grandpa were on their way again to buy baby pants so he can dance!

This time, Gram and Grandpa were stopped by the chickens who pecked at the road looking for food to better their mood.

"Please little chickens, move out of the way… it's the only thing I can think of to say. We need to get by because baby needs pants so he can dance!" Gram and Grandpa were losing their cool, wishing they were swimming in their pool!

The chickens didn't move and looking down at their feet, they continued to eat.

“I have an idea!” said Grandpa.

He went into the trunk, pulling out some bread in a hunk. Spreading the feed was quite a nice deed! With a bit of luck, the chickens moved without even a cluck! Gram and Grandpa were again on their way to buy some pants so baby can dance!

Almost to town they were stopped by the pig who rolled around in the muck with his friend the duck.

“Please get out of the PATH and go take a BATH!” Yelled Gram and Grandpa, “Don’t you know baby needs PANTS so he can DANCE?”

Gram and Grandpa did everything they could to get the pig and the duck out of the muck, again, without any luck! The pig and the duck continued to stay and that’s when Gram and Grandpa decided to pray.

“Please, Lord, give us strength so we won’t faint. Make us strong forever long. Make us patient in all that’s done and let us always remember, Jesus, your son. Give us guidance everyday and never let us go astray. Lead us now to where we go, let us get there safe in faith.”

Suddenly, God’s rainbow shined in the sky and opened up the eyes of the blind.

Getting their marching orders from the Lord, God’s word more powerful than any sword. Gram and Grandpa now knew what to do, they would run the rest of the way to get baby Paul his pants so he can dance!

Taking a short cut, they ran through the cold river, causing them to shiver. Into the tunnel, dark as can be, they ran even faster towards the light they could see. They ran through the forest and into the town without even a frown because baby needs pants so he can dance!

Into the village Gram and Grandpa found the store that sold pants so baby Paul can dance!

When they returned to the farm all was very calm. Gram and Grandpa walked into the house, waking not even a mouse! With the house full of pants, they started to dance! Waking up everyone, shouting with joy, knowing how happy they made their grand-boy. When Mommy put on baby Paul's pants, he was happy and started to dance!

Gram said laughing, "Baby no longer needs pants and look at him DANCE!"

The end

Psalm 127:3:

*Behold, children are a heritage from the Lord,
the fruit of the womb a reward.*

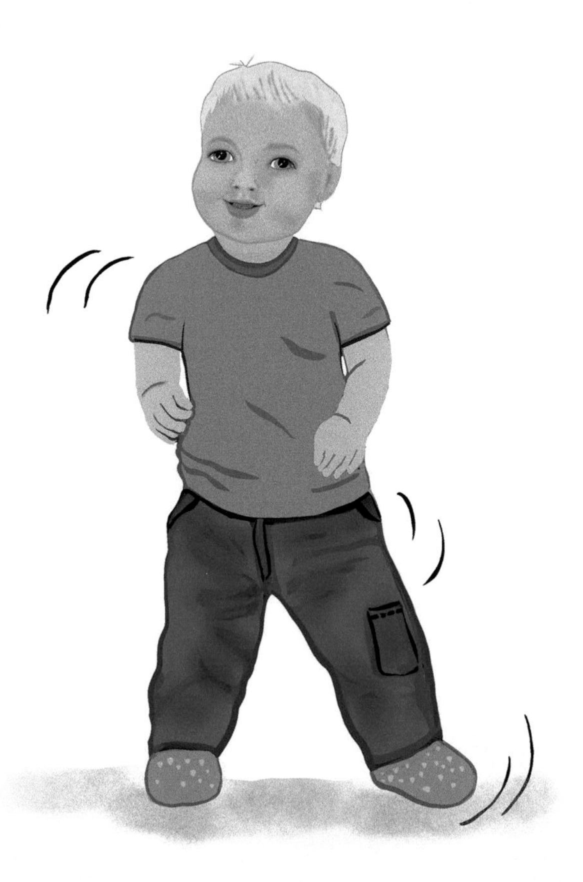

Luke 11: 9:

*And I tell you, ask and it will given to you;
seek and you will find; knock, and it will be opened to you.*

Printed in the United States
by Baker & Taylor Publisher Services

Printed in the United States
by Baker & Taylor Publisher Services